Baby Tiger and Friends Celebrate Simchat Torah

By

Lisa Ginsburg

Copyright Page

Published in the United States by Sanhedralite Editing and Publishing

ISBN: 13: 978-1499694291

Cover design and illustrations by: Malgorzata Godziuk

Edited by: Sherrie Dolby

Dedication

This book is dedicated to my parents Harriet and Michael Kovacs who have always encouraged me to pursue my dreams. I also dedicate this book to my husband Mitchel Ginsburg and daughter Shelby who have put up with my writing frenzies, sometimes at the cost of getting dinner on the table. Also, to my wonderful editor and publisher, Sherrie Dolby who has made this dream a reality.

Acknowledgements

I would like to thank the support of my editing team at Sanhedralite Editing and Publishing. Sherrie Dolby, without your support this dream would not have become a reality. I would also like to thank Malgorzata Godziuk for her beautiful illustrations. I look forward to working with you on many more books in the future.

About the Author

Lisa Ginsburg has been a Technical Writer since 2000 but her real passion is writing fiction. She received a dual Bachelor's degree in Communication and History from Michigan State University and a Master's degree in History from the University of Miami. Her "day job" is a Technical Writer with a major automotive company. She lives in the Metro-Detroit area with her husband, daughter, and Border Collie.

To learn more about the author, visit her Amazon Author Page, Sanhedralite Editing and Publishing Facebook Page, or her Personal Author Facebook Page.

Other Books by Lisa Ginsburg

Baby Tiger and Friends Celebrate Chanukah

Baby Tiger and Friends Celebrate Shabbat

Baby Tiger and Friends Celebrate Purim

Baby Tiger and Friends Celebrate Passover

Baby Tiger and Friends Celebrate Rosh Hashanah

Baby Tiger and Friends Celebrate Sukkot

Bella the Horse and the Magic Water: A Lesson About Peer Pressure

Table of Contents

Chapter One: What is Simchat Torah?

Baby Tiger and his friends Baby Elephant and Baby Bear were playing at his house one afternoon. They talked about things that they were going to be doing that weekend.

"It is so nice that it is Fall now. Mommy Bear, Daddy Bear, and I are going apple picking!" Baby Bear exclaimed.

Baby Elephant added, "I am going to help Mommy Elephant, Daddy Elephant, and Brother Elephant rake leaves."

They both looked at Baby Tiger. Baby Bear asked, "What are your weekend plans?"

"I will be going to Temple services. It is **Simchat Torah,** and we have a big celebration with lots of singing and dancing. It will be so much fun," Baby Tiger said.

Baby Bear and Baby Elephant looked at Baby Tiger curiously.

Baby Elephant turned to Baby Tiger and asked,

"What is **Simchat Torah**?"

Baby Bear added, "And what is it that you are celebrating with the singing and dancing?"

Baby Tiger told his friends, "**Simchat Torah** means 'rejoicing of the **Torah**.' The **Torah**, or the scrolled document that has the first five books of the Bible, is one of the most important books to the Jews. It has to be picked up very carefully and during a regular service, there are times when you can come up to kiss it. The **Torah** is read at almost every Jewish service as it tells important parts of our history."

Baby Elephant asked,

"If the **Torah** is special every day of the year, what exactly does **Simchat Torah** celebrate?"

Baby Tiger explained, "When we go to services at Temple, **Rabbi** Lion reads the Torah in a certain order based on days of the Hebrew calendar. In the month of Tishrei, we read the very last portion of the **Torah** before we start again at the beginning."

Baby Bear asked, "So you keep reading the **Torah** in the same order every year? What is there to celebrate about that?"

"Well," Baby Tiger told his friends, "This shows the circle of life. It means the end of one cycle of Torah readings and a beginning of new ones."

"So," Baby Bear asked, "How do you celebrate that?"

Baby Tiger went on, "On the night of **Simchat Torah**, all of the **Torah** scrolls are taken out of the **ark**, the place where they are stored during the year. People carry the **Torahs** around the Temple sanctuary and sing and dance to celebrate how important it is. A lot of us, including children, will get an **aliyah**, which is getting to say a special blessing over the **Torah**. The children will also get Israeli flags with an apple on top, and we march around the sanctuary."

Baby Elephant said, "Dancing, singing, and marching around does sound like a lot of fun!"

Baby Bear chimed in, "Why do you wave a flag with an apple on top?"

Baby Tiger then explained, "The flags represents the celebration of the **Tribes of Israel** and the apple is the symbol of the light we receive from reading the **Torah**. Sometimes candles are used instead of apples, but apples are much safer for children."

"Cool!" Baby Elephant exclaimed.

"I wish I could celebrate **Simchat Torah**," Baby Bear added.

Baby Tiger said, "Our **Simchat Torah** celebration at Temple is this weekend. You should ask your parents if you can come with us. It will be lots of fun."

Chapter Two: The Celebration Begins

Mommy, Daddy, and Baby Tiger picked up Baby Elephant and Baby Bear at their houses. Mommy Elephant and Mommy Bear agreed to meet the Tiger family at Temple later on to pick up their babies.

"Have fun!" Mommy Elephant called out as she watched Baby Elephant leave.

Mommy Bear waved to Baby Bear, Baby Elephant, and the Tiger family and said, "I will see you later. I cannot wait to hear all about your **Simchat Torah** celebration!"

Baby Tiger grinned.

"Daddy Tiger, you have an **alyiah** tonight, right?"

Daddy Tiger nodded, "I will be called up as one of the **Kohanim** this evening."

Baby Elephant asked, "What is **Kohanim**?"

Mommy Tiger explained, "There are **Three Tribes of Israel** that are represented at every service: the **Kohen**, **Levi**, and **Israelites**. All are going to be called to say a blessing over the **Torah** tonight."

Mommy Tiger, Daddy Tiger, Baby Tiger, Baby Bear, and Baby Elephant enter the sanctuary of the Temple. Everybody looks very happy.

Mr. Lion is standing at the entrance passing out flags with a white background, blue stripes on the top and bottom, and in the middle of the two stripes is a blue **Star of David**. The flags have an apple on top of them, and he gives one out to every child entering the sanctuary.

"**Chag Sameach!**" Mr. Lion greeted the Tiger family and their guests. "My wife is looking forward to celebrating the **Torah** tonight!"

Baby Bear took the flag with the apple on top from Mr. Lion. He asked, "What is **Chag Sameach**?"

"It means 'happy holiday' in Hebrew," Mr. Lion explained. He smiled and added, "Sit down and join our celebration." He pointed to where **Rabbi** Lion was standing in front of the staging area. "She is on the **bimah** now and is getting ready to start."

Rabbi Lion started reading in Hebrew from the scrolled book in front of her. Every so often, members were called up to say a blessing. After the blessing, she would read a little bit more and then another blessing was said signaling the end of the reading. At the end of each reading, everyone stood up and starting singing and dancing. A few adult members in the Temple carried a **Torah** and danced around with it. Some would take their prayer books, kiss them, and touch the **Torah** with the kissed area.

Then Daddy Tiger's name was called for his turn to say his blessing over the **Torah**. He went up to the **bimah** and recited:

"Bare khu et-Hashemhame-vo rakh,

Bless the Lord who is blessed."

Everyone answered,

"Boruch ado-noy ha-m'voroch l'olom vo-ed.

Blessed be the Lord who is blessed for all eternity."

Daddy Tiger continued:

"Baruch atah Hashem elo-haynu melech ho-olom, asher bochar bonu mikol ha-amim, v'nosan lonu es toroso. Boruch atoh ado-noy, nosayn ha-toroh.

Blessed are You, Lord our G-d, King of the universe, who has chosen us from among all the nations and given us His Torah. Blessed are You Lord, who gives the **Torah**."

Rabbi Lion read some more from the **Torah,** and Daddy Tiger stayed up on the **bimah.**

Rabbi Lion finished her reading, and Daddy Tiger took the pointer with which she was using to read the **Torah**, kissed it, and then touched the **Torah** with the pointer, symbolizing his kiss.

Daddy Tiger went on to recite:

"Baruch atah Hashem elo-haynu melech ho-olom, asher nosan lonu toras emes, v'cha-yay olom nota b'sochaynu. Boruch atoh ado-noy, nosayn ha-toroh.

Blessed are You, L-rd our G-d, King of the universe, who has given us the **Torah** of truth and planted eternal life within us. Blessed are You Lord, who gives the **Torah**."

Again, there was more singing and dancing and more members who got called up to say the special blessings.

Finally, **Rabbi** Lion announced, "Will all the children please come up to the **bimah**?"

All the children came up to the staging area. Those that knew the blessing recited it. **Rabbi** Lion read from the **Torah**.

The children said the ending blessing and then squealing with excitement, waved their flags in the air, and started marching around the entire sanctuary. Adult animals followed along, some carrying **Torah** scrolls, and marched right behind them.

8

Rabbi Lion said with joy, "We have finished our last **Torah** portion of the year! Now we begin again to show that this is like a circle: it goes round and round with neither a beginning nor an end! **Chag Sameach**! Let everybody celebrate the **Torah**!"

Everybody cheered and there was more singing, dancing, and celebrating.

Baby Elephant exclaimed, "**Simchat Torah** is so much fun!"

Baby Bear said to Baby Tiger, "Thank you for inviting me! I want to come back next year!"

Chapter Three: Until Next Time

Baby Bear, Baby Elephant, and Baby Tiger were worn out from all of that singing, dancing, and marching around. All three let out yawns. Mommy Tiger smiled.

"I think we have three very tired baby animals."

Mommy Tiger saw Mommy Bear and Mommy Elephant and waved them over.

"So," Mommy Elephant asked, "how did you like your **Simchat Torah** celebration?"

Baby Elephant smiled at her Mommy.

"It was great! We got to hear Daddy Tiger read an **aliyah,** and the children even got to say one, too!"

Baby Bear added, "And there was a lot of singing and dancing, and we marched around the whole sanctuary waving a flag with an apple on top!"

Mommy Bear smiled. "That does sound like fun!"

Mommy Bear and Mommy Elephant helped their babies get their coats on, and they started to walk out the door to go home.

Rabbi Lion came over to the group and greeted Mommy Bear and Mommy Elephant.

Baby Elephant said, "You did a great job reading the **Torah** tonight. This was a lot of fun!"

Rabbi Lion smiled. "Thank you Baby Elephant!"

She turned to Mommy Bear and Mommy Elephant.

"Your babies had lots of fun at our celebration. They are welcome to come to our Temple any time. In fact, everyone in your families should join us sometime."

Mommy Bear nodded. "That sounds like a lot of fun."

Mommy Elephant added, "I would be happy to join you at Temple for a celebration. Thank you for inviting us."

Rabbi Lion looked at Baby Bear and Baby Elephant.

"**Chag Sameach**!" she said as she waved goodbye.

Baby Bear called after **Rabbi** Lion, "**Chag Sameach** to you, too!"

Mommy and Daddy Tiger gathered theirs and Baby Tiger's coats.

"We should be leaving, too. It looks like the **Simchat Torah** celebration tired out our baby animals."

Mommy, Daddy, and Baby Tiger went home. Once they were inside, Mommy Tiger said,

"I think it is time for Baby Tiger to get ready for bed."

Mommy and Daddy Tiger helped Baby Tiger brush his teeth, wash his face, and get into his pajamas. He crawled into bed sleepily and said,

"I am very happy that I got to share a **Simchat Torah** celebration with my friends. I think Baby Bear and Baby Elephant liked learning about something new."

He let Mommy and Daddy Tiger kiss him goodnight.

"**Chag Sameach**," he said to them right before he drifted off to sleep.

Glossary

Aliyah – Special blessings of honor that are said before and after a Torah reading.

Ark- Cabinet in a Temple where the Torah is stored when not in use.

Bimah – Staging area in the main sanctuary of a Temple.

Chag Sameach – Hebrew for 'happy holiday.'

Israelite – The most common of the Three Tribes of Israel.

Kohen – One of the Three Tribes of Israel. Considered to be the highest tribe.

Levi – One of the Three Tribes of Israel, the middle tribe.

Rabbi – Leader of a Jewish congregation.

Simchat Torah – Celebration meaning 'rejoicing of the Torah' in Hebrew.

Star of David – A six-pointed star that represents Judaism.

Three Tribes of Israel – The class system among the Jews. Kohen is considered to be the highest tribe with the high priests, Levi the middle tribe, while Israelites represent the ordinary citizen.

Tishrei – Month on the Hebrew calendar that usually falls anywhere between September and October.

Torah – Scrolled book that has the five books of the Bible. It is read on most Jewish occasions and in regular services.

Recommended Reading

The Three Wisest Men by Sherrie Dolby with Sandra Haase

Al Gator And The Friendly FixerUpper Follies by Sherrie Dolby

Yoga for Children by Diane Dobler

The Legend of the Thorny Rose by Sherrie Dolby

Plucky Penguin Yearns to Fly by Sherrie Dolby

And With A Kiss, Awake by Sherrie Dolby

Short Stories for Children on a Rainy Day by Sherrie Dolby with Sandra Haase

One Last Thing...

Thank you to everybody who took the time to download and read this humble little fiction book from the Kindle market. Self-publishing is an uphill endeavor with many pitfalls and triumphs. I truly am blessed to have such a faithful readership.

Thanks also to my friends, who help me to edit my books. They too are accomplished self-publishers in their own rights and the support I receive makes the task at hand much more manageable.

Your support really does make a difference, and I read all the reviews personally so I can get your feedback and make this book even better. I would be beyond grateful to all my readers who take the time to leave me some feedback on the Kindle sales page, as reviews will go a long way toward helping me develop as a writer and continue to strive to publish the best possible books for all my readers to enjoy! I gratefully accept constructive criticism so if you find any errors or have any suggestions, please feel free to contact me at Ginsburgis@gmail.com and I will immediately correct the situation. Please leave a review on the Amazon Kindle sales page and on other book lover websites such as Goodreads and Pinterest. Thank you again for your support! I'd also love it if you would stop by Sanhedralite Editing and Publishing on Facebook and my Personal Facebook Page and leave reviews there as well.

Made in the USA
Middletown, DE
01 October 2017